RUNNING

A. M. Huff

Cover design by James M. McCracken

DEDICATION

In memory of my cousin and dear friend,
Patrick Lyman Huff.

ACKNOWLEDGMENTS

Special thanks to Michael Anne Maslow, Kathleen Mooney, Pamela Bainbridge-Cowan, Mark Fisher and James Logan for their encouragement and support.

RUNNING

When was the moment I knew I was different? I remember when I was just four I heard a song on the radio that made me cry. That's different. I mean, I don't know many other boys or girls, for that matter, who have done that at so young an age; but, true, at the time I didn't *know* I was different.

I guess I've always felt different inside, like I didn't quite belong. I don't fit in with the other guys in my senior class. Maybe that's why I started running?

I like running, especially after a good rain which it does so often here in the Willamette Valley. The air smells so fresh and clean and it feels cool against my face. I like that. I like being alone with my thoughts and being able to sort things out. I just wish it wasn't during Phys. Ed. Class.

Any other time running would relax me, but everything is a competition with Coach Brown. He hates stragglers and I'm about the worst one in the class. It's not that I can't run faster. I just don't. I don't want to be anywhere near the jocks. They're so disgusting, always laughing and talking dirty about girls. It's so stupid.

What I really hate more, though, is the thought of having to shower in the locker room. I've noticed their bodies, their muscular arms and legs, tight well-defined abs, their hairy legs and privates. I have to admit, I've never felt as comfortable in my own skin as they appear to be in theirs. If anything, I'm their polar opposite. No matter how hard I try, I have no muscle tone; hell, I don't even think I have muscles. I'm not even hairy like them. I shave my face once a week, not because I *need* to but because I want to stay in practice in case someday I *have* to shave. I'm just a scrawny, one hundred and sixty pound, seventeen-year-old and the youngest person in my class.

"Hurry up, Sticka!"

Coach Brown is yelling at me again as I head into the home stretch. There are still a few guys ahead of me. I decide to try to pass them and not come in last this time. I kick harder and faster. Take longer strides. Sweat is dripping down my face stinging my eyes. I wipe it away with the back of my hand. My lungs are starting to burn and my side aches.

I don't remember tripping or hitting the sharp pumice gravel covering the track. All I remember is lying on the ground trying to catch my breath amid the roaring laughter from the jocks huddling around above me.

Suddenly I become aware of my knees, arms and hands stinging. The pain is intense. I roll over onto my back just as Gary, one of the jocks, pushes between Donald and Jeffrey.

"Ollie, are you okay?" he asks, crouching down beside me and helping me sit up.

I look at my skinned and bloody knees, legs, arms and palms. I feel sick and a bit dizzy, but I answer him. "Yeah, I'm fine."

Coach Brown's whistle blows and the ring of jerks parts. Coach takes a look at me and frowns. "Better get to the showers and clean yourself up, Sticka. Stop by and see the nurse, too."

Wow, that's the nicest Coach has ever been to me, and that really isn't saying much. He turns around, blows his stinking whistle as loud as he can knowing everyone is standing right there. It causes me to jump, sending shooting pain throughout my body.

"Hit the showers. Class is dismissed," he yells and heads back to the Coach's Shack. Probably for another hit from his bottle of booze he doesn't think anyone knows about.

I stall, picking small bits of gravel from my injured knees and palms. Gary stays with me for which I'm glad.

"Come on, Ollie, let's get you cleaned up."

He helps me to my feet and takes my right arm, wrapping it around his neck.

"Lean on me if you need to."

I do, not because I need to but because it feels good. I like the scent of his cologne mixed with his sweat. Gary is my height, five eight. He has sandy blonde, naturally curly hair and the bluest eyes I've ever seen. He's got a nice body too, for an eighteen-year-old.

By the time we reach the locker room, most of the boys are already naked and dripping from their shower. Gary helps me to my locker and I sit on the bench in front of it. Gary's locker is across from mine so he steps across the bench and takes off his sweaty shirt. I try not to stare.

"Hey!" Donald's voice echoes throughout the tiled locker room.

I look up in time to see him strutting out of the shower, towel around his neck, his brown hair dripping, his manhood swinging freely. Our eyes met for a second.

"Like what you see, Oliver?" he asks cupping his hand over his dick and giving it a shake.

I feel my cheeks starting to turn red. I know not to answer him and quickly look down, fumbling with the laces on my shoes.

Donald grabs the towel that was beside me on the bench and dries his crotch on it.

"Here," he said throwing the towel in my face.

"No thanks, you can keep it. I'll get another one." I throw it back at him. He lets it fall to the floor and ignores me.

He leans on the locker beside Gary's.

"What's the big idea helping him?"

When Gary doesn't answer Donald nudges him in the shoulder.

"What's the big idea tripping him? That was mean, even for you." Gary snaps but keeps his voice down.

I could feel Donald looking at me again.

"But you have to admit, it was pretty funny hearing him scream like a little girl."

"No, it wasn't! You hurt him."

"It's just a few scratches. He'll get over it. Won't ya, Oliver?"

I look up and Donald is smiling at me in a pleading sort of way. I don't answer and he turns back to Gary. He's obviously mad at me because I wouldn't let him off the hook.

"You better hurry up and shower or you'll be late for next period," he tells Gary.

Without another word, Donald struts off to his locker on the other side of the room.

Gary drops his shorts and grabs his towel, wrapping it around his waist.

"Need any help?" he asks me.

"I can manage, I think. Thanks." I quickly grab a fresh towel and strip. Limping, I hurry into the showers.

Gary and I are the last two. I don't want to seem creepy, so I leave an empty shower head between us.

I turn the water on and adjust it to warm. The water still stings my hands, arms and knees. I close my eyes and carefully begin to wash my wounds with soap.

"Does it hurt much?"

I open my eyes and look at Gary. He's turned facing me, watching me gently rinse my injuries.

"A little—well, actually, a lot, but it's okay."

Gary tilts his head back under the nozzle and lets the water rinse the soap from his body. I can't help but watch the water cascade over his tanned torso and down to his groin. He looks like the sculpture of David, only better. Suddenly I become aware of my own groin and quickly shut off the shower. I grab my towel and cover up before Gary notices.

I decide not to go see the nurse. I don't want to appear weak by missing the next class. That would please Donald way too much.

When the final buzzer sounds for the day, my knees feel stiff. Even my jeans touching my skin sends shooting pain up my legs. The thought of sitting on a crowded school bus, being bounced around, knees hitting the seat in front of mine, seems too much like torture. I decide to walk home instead. It's only three miles but I know a short cut that will get me home about the same time as the bus.

"Hey, Ollie, wait up a sec.," Gary yells as I reach the side door.

I stop and wait for him to catch up.

"How're you doing? Not taking the bus?"

"No," I answer him and shake my head. "I'm a bit stiff and sore. I think I'll just walk home, today."

"Okay." He has the nicest smile. "Take 'er easy. See ya tomorrow."

I watch him rush back up the hall before turning around and leaving.

Ever since sixth grade, when I helped him with his science project, Gary has been like a friend to me. I say "like" because technically we aren't friends. We don't hang out after school or anything. We don't really have that much in common. He just doesn't go out of his way to tease me like Donald or Jeffrey or all the other guys in my class. But, I like him and he's the closest thing to a friend I have.

I make good time reaching the tracks. My knees are loosening up a lot. Walking was the right thing to do, I tell myself.

I stand at the crossing looking down the tracks. Mom has warned me several times to never walk the tracks because it isn't safe; but I know the train schedule and they only come by at 7:00 A.M. and 7:00 P.M., I have a good three hours. So, I just don't tell her I take the shortcut.

Still, there is one section of track that makes me uneasy. About halfway to my street the train tracks pass through an area where the laurel hedges on either side are so thick they form walls. The branches from the oak trees hang over the tracks forming a canopy and blocking out the sunlight. It's like walking at night even at noon. Usually I just try to think of something else and quicken my pace. Today won't be hard, because I still can't get the image of Gary's wet body out of my mind.

Walking on the steel track is like walking a tightrope but it's better than trying to walk on the unevenly spaced railroad ties. Luckily, I have good balance and can walk easily and pretty fast. I even make a game out of it sometimes to see if I can make it to my street without falling off. I've won quite a number of days.

Before I know it, I'm standing on the track at the start of the tunnel, as I call it. I usually crouch down so I can see that the tracks are clear on both sides; but today, my skinned knees are telling me to just keep walking. So I do.

I can't help thinking, as I disappear into the shadows, about the stories going around school about this stretch of tracks. Why do they have to come up now? Jeffrey, who lives on the other side of the laurel hedge on my left, claims late one night a desperate man found himself in the middle of the tunnel. He took out his pistol and blew a hole in his head. Jeffrey claims to have seen the blood splattered on the leaves of the laurel hedge and bits of scalp with hair on it. Even though I know he's lying, since how could he see blood splatters in the dark, it's still gross.

Another story, one I never heard him tell until high school so I'm even more sure it isn't true, is about two young lovers. They decide to make out on the tracks and, not being from around here, don't know the train schedule. The police took them away in large garbage bags and just let the coroner sort them out.

"Stop it! Stop it!"

"Who are you talking to?"

I jumped. My feet slip off the track, scraping the insides of my ankles, and causing me to cringe in pain.

"Who said that? Who's there?" I demand, but I'm pretty sure I recognize the voice.

I bend down a little more and see a figure of a guy standing in the middle of the track, backlit by the light at the other end of the tunnel. I glance over my shoulder and see another person a few feet behind me.

The guy in front of me laughs and I know it's Donald.

"What's the matter, Sticka?" he asks me.

"Nothing. What do you want?" I try to sound tough and unafraid even though I can feel my legs trembling already.

"Want?" Donald repeats, stepping right in front of me.

I step back only to bump against the guy behind me who has also closed in on me. Donald leans forward and whispers in my ear. I could feel his hot breath against my neck.

"I saw you checking me out in the locker room. Wanna see it again?"

"No!" I push him back. The guy behind me grabs my arms.

"Don't worry. Jeffrey wants to show you his, too."

"Yeah, Ollie, I gonna sticka you."

"I have to get home." I start to take a step around Donald but Jeffrey doesn't let go of my arms. His grip tightens and starts to hurt. "Let me go!" I pull against his grip but it's no use.

"Not until you get what's coming to you!" Donald says. They both start laughing.

"No!" I yell trying not to show how scared I am.

Suddenly I feel Donald's fist hit my left eye and I fall to the side. Jeffrey lets me fall to my knees. The sharp gravel between the ties digs into my already raw knees. I hear Donald's zipper open.

"Now keep your voice down and take it like a man!" he says. His hand grips my jaw. His fingers dig into my cheeks, prying my mouth open all the while tilting my head back.

When it's all over, I lay in the ditch beside the tracks listening to Donald's and Jeffrey's laughter and footsteps fade into the distance. Slowly I pull my briefs and jeans back up. I find my backpack beside me and then carefully climb to my feet. My legs feel like rubber and my rear hurts a bit to walk. I sling my backpack over my shoulder and continue my way home.

I don't know what I feel anymore. I want to cry. "Men don't cry!" Dad's voice echoes in my head, but right now I don't feel much like a man. It doesn't matter. I can't cry anyway.

By the time I make it home, dad is already home from work which means he's already having his second or even third beer of the night. I listen at the door before I open it. Mom is in the kitchen. Dad must be out back checking on his garden.

"I'm home!" I call out.

"You're late. Is everything okay?" Mom asks, thankfully staying out of sight in the kitchen.

"Yeah, I'm just gonna change clothes and be right down." I rush to my room, hoping that my younger sister isn't around. I'm in luck again, she's not.

Alone and safe in my room I take a look at myself in the mirror above my antique dresser. My left eye is already bruising. My lips are red and slightly swollen too. I carefully take off my jeans, noticing the oil and dirt stains in the knees. I slip off my torn briefs. For a moment I freeze. There's blood. Panic begins to set in. I quickly wad my shorts up inside my jeans and shove them into the far corner under my bed. I'll throw them away on garbage day, I tell myself. I slip into the bathroom and run a wash cloth under some warm water. Gently I wipe myself. The bleeding has stopped. The panic begins to ebb. I wipe off my other wounds and dry them with a towel.

After dressing I take a deep breath and head down to dinner. When I enter the kitchen, mom nearly drops the roast.

"What on earth happened to you?" she nearly screams. She sets the roast down on the trivet in the center of the table and rushes over to me.

"Leave the boy alone," Dad says. Mom takes a

step back. "What happened?" he asks in his usual demanding tone.

"Nothing, I just tripped and fell on the track today during P.E."

"Figures," he grumbles. "Let's eat."

The discussion about my black eye is dropped. I eat my dinner while listening to mom and dad exchange their usual barbs.

After dinner, I help clear the table and take out the garbage before going to my room to do my homework. The others retire to the living room to watch T.V. but I just want to be alone; alone with my thoughts. If only it were still light out, I'd go for a run. Instead, I turn my radio on low and try to focus on my school work.

In the morning, I shower, checking myself to be sure the bleeding really has stopped for good. Luckily, it seems to have. I pack my books into my backpack and head downstairs.

"Morning." Mom's smile turns to a frown when she sees my black eye. "I'm going to drive you and your sister to school this morning," she announces.

The panic is back instantly.

"Why?" I must have asked too quickly because mom gives me a funny look.

"I've got a few errands to run uptown and it's not too far out of the way."

"I can take the bus. I don't mind."

"Since when?" Mom gives me another one of her looks. "Or are you just feeling a bit too old to have your mother drop you off at school?"

I shrugged but give her a little smile, hoping it would be enough to keep from having her drive me to school. I need to show up for the bus. I need to show Donald and Jeffrey I'm not afraid of them.

"Okay," Mom smiled. "I'll just drop your sister off. Please, Ollie, try to be careful today." She gives my good cheek a kiss and leaves.

I skip my usual breakfast of toast and jam and head for the stop.

The bus was right on schedule. I braced myself and took a deep breath, letting it out slowly. The doors open with a hiss. I step aboard and immediately my eyes met Donald's. I look at Jeffrey seated across the aisle from him. They look smug and smile at me. Jeffrey kisses the air and grabs his crotch when I pass. Donald laughs at him. I take the empty seat behind Donald. He immediately turns sideways in his seat, leaning his back against the window. He glares at me. I ignore him.

"You better keep your mouth shut, Sticka," he hisses at me.

"That's not what you said last night," I answer back and look at him.

"Shut up or I'll blacken your other eye!"

He actually looks scared. I fight the urge to smile and I ignore him instead. Deep down I know they were probably hoping I wouldn't be at school today, and the thought of skipping did cross my mind, but I just had to go. I had to go or I would drop out for good and then my parents would find out and worse, then Gary would know what I did.

The bus stops again and Gary boards. Our eyes meet when he starts down the aisle. He's shocked, I can tell. He sits down beside Donald and turns toward me.

"What happened to your eye?"

"I fell off the tracks. I'm fine," I answer. He gives me a look that tells me he doesn't believe me and turns back around. I just can't tell him the truth. What would he think of me? Would he hate me? Or worse, would he be disappointed in me? I can't risk that. I like him too much. I settle back in my seat and stare out the window.

The day passes in a fog. I find it hard to concentrate, to focus. My mind won't stop thinking about Donald and Jeffrey, how I was scared and yet wasn't. I think about Gary, remembering his shocked expression on the bus this morning. I decide to walk home from school again. I need to go back there, to the tunnel, to where it happened.

It doesn't take as long to reach the tunnel. My heart is pounding and I'm feeling strange inside. Slowly I walk on the track, disappearing into the shadows. Halfway through, I stop. My eyes adjust to the dimness. I look around. What am I feeling? What am I doing? Suddenly I hear an answer as loud as if someone had actually said it; *you want Donald to come back.* At that moment I hear the deafening silence around me. My disquieting thoughts cease, leaving me more confused than before and totally alone.

It's a week before my black eye heals. Another for my scraped up knees and arms but at least they no longer hurt when I run. The sound of my shoes crunching the pumice gravel of the track starts to fall into a steady rhythm. I take deep breaths, trying to remember to breathe evenly and steady. I no longer care about avoiding the stupid jocks and lagging behind them. Let them talk their smut. I start running faster, for me.

Coach blows his whistle, signaling the start of the last lap. I run faster. Rounding the last bend and heading into the home stretch I pour it on, passing one and then two more boys. I come in fourth and start to walk it off.

"Keep moving!" Coach Brown yells at some of the others. "Take a walk around the track. You don't want to get leg cramps."

"Hey, Ollie," Gary yells as he trots up behind me.

"Hi," I answer and keep walking.

He doesn't say anything. He just walks beside me. A group of other guys pass us. He waits until they are out of earshot.

"Ollie, did I do something wrong?"

I look at him, at the hurt in his sad eyes.

"God, no, Gary, why would you think that?"

"Ever since the day Donald tripped you and you walked home, you seem quiet. You don't talk to me anymore. What happened?"

I suddenly feel as if someone has ahold of my heart and is squeezing it. I look into his blue eyes and become frightened. I want to tell him. I want him to know. I want him to hold me and tell me, it's okay. Yet, at the same time I'm scared. I'm afraid if he finds out he'll be disappointed in me and hate me.

I look around. We're alone. The other guys are already heading back to the locker room and we're the last to finish.

"I—we better hit the showers or we'll be late," I answer him.

"Ollie?" He's not letting it go.

I turn to him again. "I'm fine, really. I just have a lot on my mind."

He gives me that look again that tells me he doesn't believe me.

The locker room is already becoming deserted by the time we step into the showers. I leave an empty shower head between us and go about adjusting the water. Gary moves over beside me and turns on his shower. I try to ignore him.

While I rinse my hair, I have a feeling I'm being watched and look at Gary. He's facing me again, watching me. He smiles and turns back to his shower.

"Why don't you go out for track?" he asks. "It could be a lot of fun, the away meets."

"Nah, I just run for the fun of it. Besides, Coach Brown doesn't like me."

"Forget about him, you're really good. You should consider it."

I look at him. He has his eyes closed and is

letting the water run over his face, down his chest and flat stomach. I stop when I see his groin. Visions of Donald flash in my mind. I can feel his hand on my jaw again. He's gripping my head, pulling me down.

Gary clears his throat and I'm jolted back to reality, realizing that I'm still staring at him.

"Sorry," I mumble and quickly rinse off.

"Don't worry about it." I hear him say.

I wish I could.

Again I walk home, just as I have done since that day. I don't know why, but every day I find myself hoping that Donald comes back and yet I'm afraid, what if he does?

When I get to the neighbor's house I notice an unfamiliar car in the driveway. Good. Maybe no one will notice if I spend the evening in my room again. I just need time to listen to my radio and think.

When I open the front door, mom stands up from her chair in the living room. She looks directly at me.

"Ollie, come here, please."

She smiles at me. I start to feel nervous. I close the door, put my backpack down and do as I'm told. That's when I notice a man in the room. He walks over to mom's side. I give my mom a hug.

"What?"

"Do you know who this is?" she asks me, still smiling.

I look at the man. He's tall, six foot two, about eight inches taller than mom anyway. He has thinning dark brown hair that looks a little windblown and a nicely groomed, auburn beard and mustache. His eyes are dark brown behind his glasses. He's thin but a bit huskier than me.

"No," I answer.

"He's your Uncle Trevor."

I look at the man again and suddenly he looks familiar. I remember him from when I was seven or eight. Only, I always picture John Darling from Peter Pan, the boy with the top hat, round glasses and umbrella, whenever I remember him. He doesn't look at all like that kid. Still I step forward and give him a hug, all the while thinking, *who am I really hugging, Mom*?

When I let go of him and step back, he's smiling at me.

"It's been a long time, Ollie." His voice is deep yet pleasing. I like his smile, too. He is my uncle, but I'm still a bit confused. Why is he here?

"Why don't the two of you go out back and get reacquainted, while I start dinner," mom suggests. She gives me a hug and whispers in my ear. "I want you to talk to him, Ollie."

"Okay," I answer but am not sure what she means.

"Come on, Ollie," Uncle Trevor says.

I follow him out into the backyard. We walk across the lawn to the farthest corner away from the house where there are a two lawn chairs beneath a maple tree. We sit down.

"I guess this is sort of awkward for you," he begins. "I'm really a stranger to you."

"Well, sort of," I admit.

"I guess you're wondering why I'm here," he continues. He sits forward in his chair, resting his elbows on his knees and clasping his fingers in front of his mouth. "The last time I saw you, you were about what, eight? I was still in college. After I finished, I did a little traveling and then started working in San Francisco as a psychologist."

"A shrink?"

He laughs. "No, more like a counselor."

"Oh."

"Anyway, I came to see your mom and dad to tell them some news about myself. You see, Ollie, I'm gay."

He looks at me.

"Do you know what that means?"

"Yes." I nod.

"Does that bother you?"

"Not really."

"Good," he smiles. "Your mom wanted me to talk with you."

"Why?"

"Ollie, she found a pair of your shorts under your bed."

Suddenly I feel nervous and sick to my stomach. I had forgotten all about throwing them away.

"It's okay, Ollie."

No it isn't, I scream inside. "What did she say?"

"She's concerned is all. She wants to make sure you are all right."

"I'm fine," I answer. My hands start to tremble. I want to run.

"Are you sure?" he asks me.

"Yeah, I'm okay."

"Ollie," his voice is soft and nearly a whisper. "Are you gay?"

I jump up but my feet stay planted in the ground. I want to run. I don't want to have this conversation. Not with him. Not with anyone.

"I don't know," I answer.

He smiles and nods. "That's an honest answer."

"I can't talk about this. I've got to go."

Before he can say another word to stop me, I run around the house and to the street out front. Soon the rhythmic sound of my footfalls on the sidewalk echoes up to my ears and I begin to think.

Oh god, how long has mom known about my underwear?

Surely she's known for some time. She found your bloody shorts and called her brother for help. He dropped everything and flew up here to shrink your head

Oh god, he said he's gay. Was that just to get me to say I am? Does Mom think I am? Does Dad?

Don't be stupid, of course they do! Everybody knows what you did. You aren't fooling anyone.

"No! No! No! I'm not. I'm not gay!" I suddenly realize I just spoke out loud. I look around.

Thank heaven the sidewalk is deserted.

Instead of feeling relaxed, I feel nauseous. I want to throw up but I haven't anything to throw up. I skipped lunch today. I keep running, not heading for anywhere particularly, just anywhere but home. I can't go back there, not yet, maybe not ever.

I run until my lungs burn and my side aches. I slow to a walk. Sweat is dripping down my spine clear to my underwear. I hate that feeling.

When did life become so complicated? Why me? Why can't I go back to being eight again, when my concerns were about not missing the next episode of Lassie and Saturday morning cartoons? Life was so much easier then. I didn't have to think about grown up things.

Are you gay? Uncle's voice rings in my ears.

I don't know! I don't know!

I wipe the sweat from my cheeks, or are they tears? I think of Gary, of wanting him to take me in his arms and tell me it's going to be all right. No, I mean Mom. I want her to tell me, it's okay, but I'm afraid. I don't want her to look at me the way she did when my older sister became pregnant when she was my age. I don't want her to be disappointed in me.

I walk and before I realize it I'm standing in front of my house again. Uncle Trevor's car is still in the driveway next to dad's. The lights are still on in the living room. I start to tremble again.

Mom looks at me when I walk into the house.

She smiles.

"Have a good run?"

"Yeah," I answer. I notice dad is standing by the fireplace pretending to look at something, anything but me.

"I'm not hungry. I think I'll just take a shower and go to bed. Good night."

I can't believe they let me go without more of a fight. I shower and put my pajama shorts on, then slip into bed.

I'm almost asleep when I hear a faint tapping on my door. I roll over onto my back just as mom opens the door. The light from the hallway illuminates her auburn hair like a halo.

"May I come in?" she asks but doesn't wait for an answer. She walks over and sits down on the edge of my bed. She gently strokes my hair and puts her hand on my cheek. She smiles. "Ollie, please, I want you to know that I love you, no matter what. I just want you to be happy."

"What about dad?"

She looks at the doorway. "Don't worry about him. He'll be fine. It's you I'm worried about. Please, talk to your uncle. Stay close to him. Promise me?"

I don't know what to say, what to think. "I'll try."

"Good," she smiles. "He'll be here for a couple days. Maybe you could spend the afternoon with him or go to the park or something."

"Okay," I agree because I don't know what else to

say.

She kisses my forehead and starts to leave. Pausing at the door she looks back. "You'll always be my son and I will always love you, Ollie, no matter what."

"I love you, Mom."

See, she thinks you are, so that means you're gay.

No! I'm not! Stop saying that!

I roll over and face the wall. I don't know when I finally fell asleep. The next morning I awake to the chirping of birds outside my window. I look at the clock on my desk and jump out of bed. I over slept. Someone must have turned off my alarm. I quickly dress, grab my backpack and rush out of my room.

"I'm late!" I shout when I reach the living room. "I gotta run or I'll miss the bus."

"Ollie, stop!" Mom yells at me before I get out the front door.

"What? I'm gonna miss the bus."

"I already called and had you excused from school for the day."

"What?" I instantly think of Gary.

"I want you to spend the day with your Uncle Trevor."

I return to my room and plop my backpack on my desk. I turn my radio on and then sit on the floor, leaning against my bed. I don't know what I feel. I should be happy not having to go to school. It means one less Phys. Ed. Class. Yet at the same time, I think of not seeing

Gary and even Donald and I feel sad. Does that make me gay?

No. I think back to eighth grade when I had a crush on Angela. She sat at the desk across the aisle from me. She was cute, light brown hair, hazel eyes, pink cheeks. She only had eyes for Brandon. The two of them would sneak down to the basement of the gym and kiss. So, when Sandy asked me to be her boyfriend, I agreed. We joined them on a "double date." But when I was kissing her, I was really wanting to kiss *Brandon*—no, Angela! Why did I think that?

Because it's true. You wanted to kiss Brandon and you know it.

No, Angela. I wanted to kiss Angela. Why do you keep saying that?

Why are you denying it?

A knock on my bedroom door jolts me out of my argument with myself. I look up just as the door opens. It's Uncle Trevor.

"Morning, Ollie. Mind if I come in?"

"Sure." I shrug and pull myself up, sitting down on my bed. I turn the radio down.

"So, how are you this morning?" he asks. He pulls out the chair by my desk and turns it around to face my bed. He sits down.

"I'm okay." I start to feel butterflies in my stomach again.

"What would you like to do today? Do you want to go for a drive? We could go to the beach; it's only an hour and a half drive."

"I guess." I answer him.

"Grab your jacket and let's go."

Two hours later, Uncle Trevor pulls into the D River State Recreational parking lot overlooking the beach and ocean in Lincoln City. The sky is clear. It's warm but there is a gentle breeze blowing. I won't need my jacket after all. Uncle Trevor suggests we go for a walk on the sand, so we get out of the car. Since it's a school day, there aren't but a handful of people about and they are a long way up the beach. We walk in the opposite direction, toward the south.

The sand gives under my feet, some finding its way into my shoes. I hate that feeling. We stop and I take them off, shaking the sand from my socks before stuffing them inside my shoes. I tie my shoelaces together and sling my shoes over my shoulder.

"Have you given anymore thought to our conversation last night?" Uncle Trevor starts.

Of course I have. That's all I've been able to think about. "Some," I answer.

"You do realize, Ollie, whatever you tell me will stay between us."

I look at him. No, I didn't realize that. I thought you would report everything I say back to my parents.

"You mean you won't tell my mom and dad?"

"No, not a word. So, do you want to talk about…whatever you're feeling?"

I return to looking at my feet while we walk.

"I'm not very good at talking about my feelings."

"I see."

"But, can I ask you a question?"

"Sure."

"When did you know you were gay?"

"Oh, I would have to say I've known since before they adopted the title Gay. Before then people called people like me queers, fags, homos, and all sorts of less than flattering names."

"But how old were you? I mean, how did you know?"

"I guess I always knew I was attracted to boys. I tried to have girlfriends because that's what guys are supposed to have and do, but I never felt any real connection; certainly not any romantic connection with them. It wasn't until I went away to college that I had my first boyfriend. It was in the mid-seventies, the age of the discos and the dawn of the Gay Movement."

"Did Grandma and Grandpa know?"

"No," he answers shaking his head. His expression changes. "If they did, they never let on. They never talked about it."

"Do they know now?"

"Yes." He nods.

"How did they take it?"

He takes a deep breath and lets it out slowly. He looks a little uncomfortable. Maybe I asked too much.

"Your grandmother pretends to be okay with it," he finally says, "but your grandfather, let's just say we aren't on speaking terms and haven't been for years for different reasons."

"Oh, I'm sorry."

"Don't be," he says and gives me a smile. "It's his problem, not mine."

We walk a little farther and then get our feet wet in the surf. The water is still ice cold so we don't linger too long. Uncle Trevor decides it's time for some lunch. We drive down past the outlet mall and find a small, quiet, out-of-the-way restaurant that serves barbequed ribs and chicken.

We settle into a corner table away from the other two people in the restaurant. A radio is playing some oldies. Uncle Trevor cocks his head and smiles while he listens.

"This was on the first album I ever bought," he tells me.

I don't answer. I mean, what can I say, that's nice? I look at the menu.

After we order and the waitress brings us our Cokes, Uncle Trevor gets a serious look on his face.

"So, you graduate in a couple months," he says.

"Actually, there are fifty-five more school days."

He smiles. "What are you going to do then? College?"

"No, Dad says he can't afford to pay for college. If I want to go, I'll have to figure out a way to pay for it myself. I don't know how I'm supposed to do that since all of the financial aid forms want his income information and he refuses to give it. So, I guess college is out."

"There has to be another way, if it's something you really want."

"It's okay. I don't even know what I want to do. I mean, I thought about being an English teacher, but I don't know anymore."

"Well, don't give up. It could still happen for you."

The waitress brings our orders and leaves. I watch Uncle Trevor while he eats. He is so neat and proper, holding his fork just so and being careful not to get barbeque sauce all over himself. I try to copy him and be neat but somehow I still end up with sauce on my hands and face.

After we finish, we walk back to the car. We head off down the coast highway toward Depoe Bay. He says he hasn't been there since he was my age. He wants to see if they still offer boat rides out into the ocean.

While he drives, I look out the window at the passing scenery. I know what's coming next and I start to feel a bit uneasy.

"Ollie,"

Oh no, here it comes.

"Your mom told me about your black eye. You told her you tripped and fell." He glances at me and gives me the look that says he doesn't believe me either. "What really happened?"

Do I dare tell him the truth?

"I did trip and fall during Phys. Ed.; or, actually, I

was tripped. This guy in my class, Donald, tripped me. I scraped up my knees, arms and hands really good."

"What about your eye?"

"When I was walking home, he stopped me and punched me."

"Why would he do that?"

I feel my stomach tighten and panic creeping up inside. I look at him. He's focused on the road.

"I need some air," I say.

"I'll pull over at Boiler Bay," he says after we pass the sign that warns us the turn off is one mile ahead.

The parking lot is deserted. I'm relieved. We get out of the car and walk over to a picnic table away from the others, just in case someone stops. We sit down across the table from each other. I'm still feeling nervous and sick.

"Ollie, you can tell me. It's okay."

I look at him. How can I tell you when I'm not even sure myself; I mean how I feel.

"You have to promise you won't tell my parents."

"I promise."

"I took the shortcut home, the railroad tracks. Mom's told us all a million times not to walk on the tracks because it's dangerous but I know when the trains come and it's safe. Anyway, there's this one part where the trees and bushes are so thick it's dark. I usually walk fast and it's no problem. But that day, Donald and his buddy Jeffrey were hiding there waiting for me. Donald said I was checking him out in the locker room. I wasn't.

He struts around naked. Anyway, he wanted me to do something to him. I told him, no, and that's when Jeffrey grabbed my arms and Donald punched me. That's how I got the black eye."

Uncle Trevor is staring at me as if he can see deep inside me.

"Did they do something to you?" His voice is gentle.

I nod, keeping my eyes turned down to avoid his.

"How do you feel about what happened?"

"I don't know. I'm just confused."

"Confused?"

"I mean, when they were—doing what they did, I got aroused. It hurt but at the same time it felt good. I don't like either one of those guys but I can't stop thinking about them, especially about Donald."

"What do you mean?"

"I mean, I think about what he did, what he made me do to him, and—"

I look up at Uncle Trevor. He's still watching me intensely. It makes me more nervous.

"Do you think that makes me gay?"

"That all depends, Ollie. Are you attracted to him?"

"No! I mean, sort of, I don't know."

"What about girls? Do you have a girlfriend?"

Why do I get the feeling he already knows the answer to that? "No."

"How do you feel about that?"

"I'm fine. I never really think about it."

"Do you *want* a girlfriend?"

"To be honest, no."

"Ollie, no one can tell you, you're gay. That is something you have to figure out on your own. Either you are attracted to women or you're attracted to men. I can only tell you, for me, ever since I can remember I've always been sexually attracted to men. For me, there was no choosing. You might even say I was born gay."

That's how I feel. All of the sudden, I don't feel anxious anymore.

"No matter what, Ollie, don't worry about what anyone else thinks. You can't control that. If they have a problem with it, that's on them, not you. Does that make sense?"

"Yeah," I answer. "Thank you."

"Let's skip the boat ride and head back home," he suggests.

"Sounds good."

We get up and he walks around the table. He gives me a hug and it feels as if a weight has been lifted off me. I hug him back and just enjoy the embrace. I feel safe. It then occurs to me that dad doesn't hug me anymore. When did he stop? I try to remember.

That evening mom asks me to help her in the kitchen. She hands me a bowl of potatoes and the peeler. I sit down at the small table against the wall while she bastes the chicken.

"So, how did your day with your Uncle Trevor

go?"

"Okay."

"Just okay?"

"Yeah. We had a nice lunch and visit."

"Good."

I look at her and she smiles.

"Ollie, I want you to keep in touch with him. If you ever need to talk to someone, you can talk to him. Okay?"

"Okay, I will." I assure her.

It was hard going back to school after Uncle Trevor's visit. He left early in the morning but stopped by my bedroom to say good bye. He gave me his phone number, mailing address and even his e-mail address so I could call or write him whenever I needed. I actually hated to see him go.

I love the sound of pumice rock beneath my feet. I keep picturing the expression on Coach Brown's face. He was so surprised when I told him I wanted to go out for track. He smiled like he was genuinely pleased. That's not a look I'm used to seeing from him.

"Hey, Ollie, wait up a bit," Gary calls to me after I finish my laps. "Missed you last Friday, were you sick?"

"No. My Uncle was visiting from San Francisco. Mom got me excused from school so I could spend the day with him."

"Cool. What did you do?"

"We drove to the coast and we talked a lot."

"Did you talk about me?"

I looked at him. He wasn't looking at me. "No. But you did cross my mind a time or two."

"Really?" he smiled.

"Yeah," I answered and nodded. "Gary, I need to tell you something."

"Okay."

We stop walking around the track and head off onto the field. We walk over to the tall, green, plywood wall that's used as a backstop for soccer practice. We sit on the ground, resting our backs against it.

"What is it?" he asks.

"I know we aren't technically friends and all, but I think of you as one and I'll understand if you don't want anything to do with me after what I am about to tell you."

There's a look of confusion in his beautiful blue eyes. My heart beats faster. I'm not sure if it's because I'm afraid or because he's just so handsome.

"Gary, I'm gay."

He's eyes widen while he looks at me. He looks away for a moment and then looks back. "Is that why you've been so distant?"

"Yes."

He looks away again and I start to feel nervous. Did I say too much?

"Is that the only reason?"

"No. You remember the day Donald tripped me and I walked home?"

"Yeah." He nods his head.

"He and Jeffrey attacked me. They did something to me and I was afraid if you found out you'd hate me."

"What did they do?"

"They raped me." I can't believe I just said the word. The shock on Gary's face is nothing compared with the way I feel inside at this very moment.

"Are you serious?"

"Yes," I answer. I feel tears beginning to well up in my eyes. No. I can't cry in front of him.

Suddenly he reaches over and wraps his arms around me. "I'm so sorry."

I hug him and begin to cry.

I don't know how long he held me or how long I cried, but it felt good to be in his arms. I finally ease up on my hold and he does the same. I pull back and wipe the tears from my cheeks with my sweatshirt.

"I'm glad you told me," he said.

I look at him. "So you don't hate me?"

"No." He shakes his head. "Maybe we could start hanging out?"

"Really? I'd like that."

"Me too."

We both stand up at the same time.

"I have some other news for you. I told Coach I'm going out for track."

Gary smiles. "Good for you!" He gives me another hug and to my surprise a kiss on the cheek.

"We better hit the showers or we'll miss our next class."

When we reach the locker room, the showers are full. Donald struts out of the shower in his usual glory. I don't even look, but I can see he notices and actually looks disappointed. I undress and follow Gary into the showers.

ABOUT THE AUTHOR

A. M. Huff was born and raised in Oregon. He currently resides in Central Oregon where he spends his days writing and enjoying the relaxed life that comes with living in a small town. He is a member of the Northwest Independent Writers Association that is working to improve the quality of independently published books.

For more about the author, visit his website: amhuff.com

If you enjoyed *Running* please feel free to leave a review on Amazon or Goodreads. Thank you.